JUDY MOODY AND FRIENDS

Countdown to Trouble

Megan McDonald

illustrated by Erwin Madrid

based on the characters
created by Peter H. Reynolds

CANDLEWICK PRESS

CONTENTS

BOOK 1

Frank Pearl in The Awful Waffle Kerfuffle   1

BOOK 2

Stink Moody in Master of Disaster   65

BOOK 3

Triple Pet Trouble   129

Frank Pearl in
The Awful Waffle Kerfuffle

For Richard

M. M.

For my nieces, Melanie and Mariel

E. M.

CONTENTS

CHAPTER 1

The Fro-Yo Yo-Yo Contest 5

CHAPTER 2

The Kooky Cookie Contest 23

CHAPTER 3

The Awful Waffle Kerfuffle 43

CHAPTER 1
The Fro-Yo Yo-Yo Contest

Frank Pearl walked the dog down Jumper Street. He walked the dog down Croaker Road. He walked the dog past Judy Moody's house.

"What's up, Frank?" Judy called.

"I'm walking the dog," said Frank.

"But there's no dog," said Judy. "How can you walk the dog without a dog?"

Frank held up his brand-new, super-sleek Whizz Master 5000 yo-yo. It was Fast with a capital *F*. "Walking the Dog is a yo-yo trick."

"When you're done walking your yo-yo," Judy asked, "want to go look for turtles?"

"Can't. I have to Rock the Baby," said Frank.

"Baby? What baby?"

"Then I have to Skin the Cat."

"More yo-yo tricks?" said Judy.

Frank nodded. "I'm on my way to the frozen-yogurt shop. Today is the Fro-Yo Yo-Yo contest."

"Whoa-whoa. Wait a minute. You hate contests."

"I hate *not winning* contests," said Frank. "Just once I want to be the best-ever, blue-ribbon, one-of-a-kind winner at something."

Frank walked the dog all the way to Fro-Yo World, with Judy right beside him.

Swoosh! Whoosh! Doing! Boing! Fro-Yo World was full of Atom Smashers. It was full of Flying Saucers. It was full of Time Warps and Tidal Waves.

"Ricky Ricasa!" said Frank, pointing.

"No way!" said Judy. "Who's Ricky Ricasa?"

"Mr. Whizz Master himself. Fastest Flying Trapeze in the East."

"Rare!" said Judy.

"He's going to show us his famous tricks before the contest. The kid with the best yo-yo trick gets to name a fro-yo flavor."

Just then, Ricky Ricasa got out his Super Deluxe Titanium Series 3 Orbiter.

It gleamed. It glistened. It glinted in the light.

Swish! Swash! Whizzzz! That yo-yo popped up off the ground. That yo-yo flew through the air. That yo-yo spun and swung and twisted and looped.

Brain Twister!

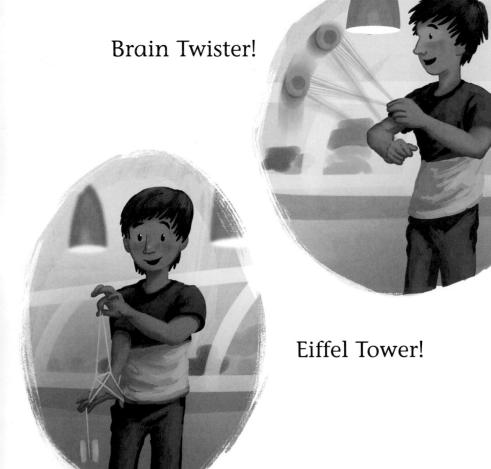

Eiffel Tower!

Punching Bag!

When the show was over, the crowd
went wild.

"Warm up those yo-yos," said Ricky
Ricasa. "Gimme what you got."

A kid with red hair went
Around the World.

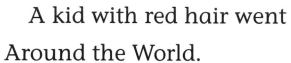

A girl with ponytails
Walked the Tightrope.

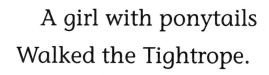

A guy with a frog voice
showed off a Shooting Star.

Then Paisley Parker did the
Boingy Boing—with sound effects!
The Boingy Boing was Expert Level
Three. She started with a Split Bottom
Mount. Then she bounced and
boinged that yo-yo back and forth
more than sixteen times!

WHOOSH!

At last it was Frank's turn. "My trick is called the Flying Skunk. It's a cross between the Shooting Star and the Flying Saucer."

Frank let his yo-yo drop to the floor. He wound the string around and around. He pulled back and *WHAMMO*. His yo-yo hung in the air for one, two, three seconds, spinning madly. Lights blinked and flashed like fireworks.

That skunk was flying!

At last, Frank flicked his finger to call that skunk home. But the yo-yo spun out of orbit. It zigged. It zagged. That yo-yo went cuckoo!

"Duck!" Judy yelled.

Yikes! The runaway string wrapped around Frank's head. The string looped over his ear. The string tangled up in his glasses. Frank's glasses crashed to the floor. *Smasheroo!*

He put them back on. The blinking yo-yo still dangled from his glasses. The crowd roared.

"Looks like this young man got skunked," Ricky Ricasa teased. "Good trick. Keep working on that landing."

Frank plopped beside Judy. "The skunk stunk," said Frank. *"And* I broke my glasses."

"You could still win," said Judy.

"Drumroll, please," said Ricky Ricasa. "And the winner is . . . everybody! Line up for your *free* mini fro-yo."

"But who gets to name that fro-yo flavor?" asked Frank.

"That would be Paisley Parker for the Boingy Boing!" Everybody clapped.

"Oh, man! I wanted to name that yogurt the Flying Skunk," Frank told Judy.

"Skunk fro-yo? P.U.," said Judy.

Frank stepped up to get his free mini cone. It sure was mini. "They should name this Thumbelina," said Frank.

Paisley Parker was holding a not-mini, double-decker, triple-swirl fro-yo. It was drip-drip-drippy.

"Your trick was awesome," said Frank. "And your dismount? Wow. It was like a yo-yo somersault."

"Thanks," said Paisley. Her fro-yo dripped all over the floor.

"Don't you like your fro-yo?" Judy asked.

"I'm allergic," said Paisley. "But I still have to think up a name for it."

"I'll help," said Frank. He took a lick. He took another lick. Lick-lick-lick-lick-lick.

"Any ideas?" asked Paisley.

"Don't say Flying Skunk," said Judy.

"I'd call this the . . . Yo-Yoing,
Double-Boing, Banana-Split-
Destroying Somersault." *Slurp!*

CHAPTER 2
The Kooky Cookie Contest

"Guess what," Frank told Judy. "I'm going to enter Cookie in a contest."

"A cookie contest?" said Judy. "Let's make snickerdoodles!"

"Snickerdoodle," said Cookie the parrot.

"No, I'm going to enter Cookie, *my parrot,* in a contest."

"What about yo-yos?" Judy asked.

"I was a yo-yo to think I could win a yo-yo contest," said Frank.

"Frank's a yo-yo," said Cookie.

"Am not!" said Frank.

"Frank eats paste," said Cookie.

"My sister taught her *that* one," said Frank.

"Beddy-bye. Nighty-night," said Cookie.

"It's not bedtime," said Frank. "Time to learn a new trick."

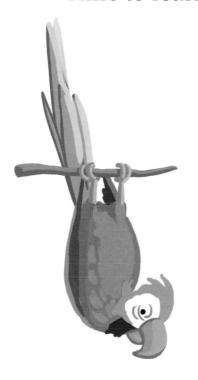

"What tricks can she do?" Judy asked.

"She can hang upside down. She can waddle her butt to music. And when she hears the vacuum cleaner, she says, 'Frank's a poopy head.'"

"Funny! Do that one," said Judy.

"The contest is called Pets Are Family. Cookie's trick has to show that she's a special part of my family."

Cookie hopped onto Frank's arm. Frank held out a peanut.

"Gimme kiss," said Frank.

"Waak!" Cookie ruffled her feathers.

"Gimme kiss," said Frank.

"Waak!" Cookie bobbed her head up and down.

"Cookie. You can do this," said Frank. "Gimme kiss."

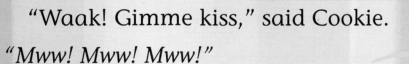

"Waak! Gimme kiss," said Cookie.
"Mww! Mww! Mww!"

Judy clapped. "She did it! She even made funny smooching sounds."

"Good girl," said Frank. He gave her a peanut.

"Good girl," said Cookie.

On the day of the contest, Judy and Rocky met Frank at Fur & Fangs.

"There's a parrot here named Rocky!" said Rocky.

"Dirty bird. Dirty bird," said Cookie.

"What's the prize, anyway?" asked Rocky.

"Who cares?" said Frank. "Just once I want to win a contest like you guys!"

"What did I ever win?" asked Rocky.

"You won a trick deck of cards at the House of Magic."

"I'm a pirate," said Cookie. "Cap'n Cookie."

"Stop that," said Frank.

"Stop that," said Cookie.

Frank frowned at his parrot. "And Judy won a famous pet contest," he said.

"My *cat* won," said Judy.

"You still got your picture in the paper," Frank said.

Judy held up her elbow. "I got my *elbow* in the paper."

"Welcome to Pets Are Family Day!" said Mrs. Birdwistle, the pet store lady. "And a warm welcome to our furry and feathered friends!"

"Frank eats paste," said Cookie.
Everybody cracked up.

Luna, a cat wearing
glasses, pretended to
read.

A guinea pig named
Dorothy played
Scrabble. She nudged
the letters *P-I-G* with her nose!

There was even a
dog named Bo who
could take out the
trash.

Everybody clapped. Bo got so excited
that he knocked over the trash can!
"Sorry about that," said his owner.

"No worries," said Mrs. Birdwistle.
"We'll get this cleaned up in no time."

At last it was Cookie's turn.

"Dirty bird!" said Cookie. "Dirty bird!"

Cookie perched on Frank's arm. "Hi. My name is Frank Pearl and this is Cookie. Our trick is called Gimme Kiss."

Frank held out a peanut. "Ready? Gimme kiss."

"Lu, lu, lu, lu," said Cookie.

"Not lulu," said Frank. "C'mon, Cookie. You can do this. Gimme kiss."

RrrooaaRR! Vacuum cleaner! Somebody turned on the vacuum to clean up the trash.

"Frank is a poopy head!" sang Cookie. She raced up and down Frank's arm. "Poopy head!" Cookie hopped up onto Frank's head, flapping her wings wildly. "Frank is a big sister." The crowd went crazy.

"The vacuum freaks her out," said
Frank. He rushed Cookie out the door.
Judy and Rocky ran after him.

"*You're* a poopy head," Frank said to Cookie.

"It wasn't her fault," said Judy. "It was the vacuum cleaner."

"There goes another contest down the tubes."

"Down the tubes!" said Cookie.

"Cookie, don't you get it?" Frank asked. "I'm mad at you. Don't say a word. Not one more word."

Cookie ruffled her feathers. Cookie bobbed her head. Cookie wiggled her butt.

"Gimme kiss!" said Cookie. *"Mww! Mww! Mww!"*

CHAPTER 3
The Awful Waffle Kerfuffle

Frank pointed to the poster in the school lunchroom. His mouth fell open. A glob of ABC sandwich fell out.

"Gross!" said Judy Moody and Jessica Finch.

"Gross!" said Amy and Rocky.

THE GREAT THIRD-GRADE BREAKFAST BASH AND WAFFLE-OFF!

This Saturday in the school cafeteria

• Families welcome •

• Prizes for best waffles •

• Proceeds go to third-grade field trip •

"Look! It's the Great Third-Grade Breakfast Bash! We get to come to the cafeteria on Saturday with our families and eat breakfast."

"What's so great about breakfast?" asked Rocky.

"It's only the most important meal of the day," Jessica Finch said.

"Breakfast tastes like pencil shavings," said Rocky.

"But this year it's a Waffle-Off," said Frank. "To raise money for our third-grade field trip."

"So we can go to the Smelly Jelly Bean factory!" said Judy. "Where they make weird flavors of jelly beans, like toothpaste and rotten eggs."

"What's a Waffle-Off?" asked Amy.

"The Waffle-Off is the best contest ever," said Frank. "It's to see who can make the best, most amazing waffle."

"They give out blue ribbons for all kinds of waffles," said Jessica. "Like Most Blueberries, Whipped Creamiest, and Best Use of Sprinkles."

"I'm going to win," said Frank. "I can feel it!"

"Are you off your waffle, Frank?" asked Judy.

"You can't even cook," Rocky said. "Can you?"

"Parents make the waffles," Jessica told them. "All you have to do is dress up your waffle fancy with whipped cream and sprinkles and stuff. Then Mr. Todd gives out ribbons before they get eaten."

Frank and his friends got quiet, dreaming about waffles.

"I've got a great idea for my waffle!" said Frank.

"Is your waffle a *sandwich*?" Judy asked. "Mine is going to be a whipped-cream sandwich."

"Does your waffle play sports?" Rocky asked. "Mine is going to play sports. And it's not going to taste like pencil shavings."

"My idea snap-crackle-pops! My idea will *blow* your mind. It's all about the *fizz*-i-cality. Just you wait."

At last it was Saturday. "Welcome to the Great Third-Grade Breakfast Bash," said Mr. Todd. "Thanks for coming to our Waffle-Off! I hope you're all ready to *break an egg*." Everybody laughed.

"Ready, set, waffle!" Moms and dads poured batter onto sizzling waffle irons. *Pssh!* Fluffy, puffy golden waffles!

Judy's waffle sandwich was held up
with pizza tables.

Rocky's waffle looked like a soccer ball.

Amy's waffle had her name spelled in blueberries.

Then came the Piggy on a Pillow, made by Jessica A. Finch. A puffy pink cloud of whipped cream floated on top of her waffle. It was sprinkled with sugar glitter. On top was a sugar-dusted candy piggy with rosy-red cheeks.

"I can win for the pinkest or prettiest waffle," said Jessica.

"Or piggiest," Judy teased.

Frank had hidden his top-secret, none-of-your-beeswax waffle under a cake dome. "Ta da!" said Frank. "Presenting"—he lifted the lid—"the Super-Amazing Exploding Volcano Waffle!" A hill, a mountain, a tower of brown jelly beans rose up from that waffle like a volcano. The Mount Vesuvius of all waffles.

Marshmallow Fluff spewed from a hole in the top. *Pop, pop, fizz, fizz.* Fizzlers, wizzlers, and sizzlers popped and exploded like lava.

"Wait till Mr. Todd sees this!" said Frank. "Blue ribbon, here I come!"

Then, all of a sudden, the fizzlers fizzled and the wizzlers melted into the sizzlers. Rainbow-colored lava oozed down the jelly-bean mountain. *Plop!* The glop hit the floor in one giant gluppy glob of gloop.

"OOH! Gross! Bluck!" said all the kids.

"Mount Vesuvius meltdown!" said Frank.

Stink came running over to see.

"What's all this waffle kerfuffle?" asked Mr. Todd.

"It's Frank's Super-Amazing Exploding Waffle," said Judy.

"Super-Amazing *Disaster* Waffle," said Frank. "It was supposed to be an exploding volcano. But the jelly beans caved in. And all the Pop Rocks ran together. Now it just looks like a giant mud pie."

He ran to grab a towel from the kitchen. On his way, he passed the prize table full of ribbons. Shiny blue ribbons that called out MOST! BEST! BIGGEST! FANCIEST! He would never win the contest now. He would no-way no-how be taking home a ribbon.

When he came back with the towel, Frank could not believe his eyes. There, gleaming in a beam of sunlight, was none other than one of those very same big shiny blue prize ribbons. The ribbon was on *his waffle*. The Mount Vesuvius Meltdown.

Stink yelled and pointed. "Hey, Frank! You won! You won the awful waffle contest!"

"But *not* for being awful," said Judy.
Frank leaned in and read the ribbon.
ONE OF A KIND! "I won? I actually won
a contest? With a real blue ribbon?"
He looked at Mr. Todd.

"Your waffle is in a class by itself, Frank."

Frank stuck the blue ribbon on his shirt and grinned.

"It's one of a kind," said Mr. Todd. "Just like you."

Stink chewed on a jelly bean from Frank's waffle. "Hey!" He made a face. "It tastes like pencil shavings."

"Told you!" said Rocky.

"I like it! Got any more?"

Frank laughed. "Ha, ha. Those are Smelly Jelly jelly beans. They *look* like maple syrup, but the flavor is pencil shavings."

"Clever," said Mr. Todd. "I like how you tied it into our class field trip to the Smelly Jelly Bean factory."

"Too bad you don't win *money* with that ribbon," said Rocky. "Then you could buy more Smelly jellies."

Stink reached into his pocket. He pulled out a dollar bill. "One dollar! I'll give you one whole dollar bill for the one-of-a-kindest, awfulest, most delicious waffle in the world!"

"Sold!" said Frank.

Stink Moody
in Master of Disaster

CONTENTS

CHAPTER 1

The Sherlock-Holmes Comet 69

CHAPTER 2

Master of Disaster 91

CHAPTER 3

Albert Einstink 111

CHAPTER 1
The Sherlock-Holmes Comet

Judy and Stink were sleeping out in the backyard. Judy and Stink were stargazing. Judy and Stink were searching the sky for comet P/2015 OZ4. The Sherman-Holm comet. Stink called it the Sherlock-Holmes comet.

The night sky looked like the *Starry Night* painting, only better. "No blinking, Stink," Judy told him.

"A comet is a once-in-a-lifetime thing. No way would you want to miss it."

Stink tried not to blink. But thinking about blinking just made him blinkier.

"Sure is dark out here," said Stink.

"That's because it's nighttime, Stink."

"Sure is quiet out here," said Stink.

"That's because it's nighttime, Stink."

Judy pointed to a band of stars that looked like a giant brushstroke across the sky. "That's the Milky Way," said Judy.

"Hey! There's the Big Dipper. And the Little Dipper. And the Medium Dipper."

"And there's Wynken, Blynken, and Nod," said Judy.

"For real?" asked Stink.

"Gotcha!" said Judy, laughing herself silly.

It was dark for a long time. It was quiet for a long time.

73

"They should call this star-*waiting*," said Stink.

"Good things come to those who wait, Stink."

"Says who?"

"Abe Lincoln. The ketchup bottle. Mom and Dad."

While he waited, Stink dumped out his backpack. "Star book. Star map. Star finder. Flashlight. Toilet-paper-tube telescope, and . . . my Star Talker DL7."

Stink pressed a button.

"The full moon in March is called a Worm Moon."

Stink pressed the button again.

"A star in Draco, the Dragon, was used by ancient Egyptians to build pyramids."

Stink pressed the button again.

"The full moon in March is called a Worm Moon."

Stink pressed the button again.

"The full moon in March is called a Worm Moon."

Judy put her hands over her ears. "Make that thing stop! All you need for stargazing is your eyes, Stink. And a little P and Q."

"P and Q?"

"Peace and quiet."

Stink opened his *Big Head Book of Stars.* Stink held his star map up to the sky. He turned it this way and that.

Judy watched the twinkling stars in the velvet sky and waited.

Stink spun his star finder to August.

Stink squinted one eye and looked through his toilet-paper-tube telescope.

Stink studied his star map. He
found the Eagle,

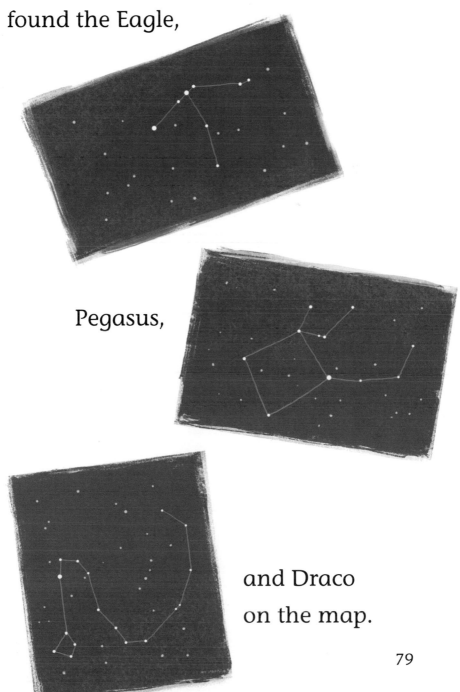

Pegasus,

and Draco
on the map.

79

Judy studied the night sky. She found the Swan, the tail of Scorpius, and the Summer Triangle in the sky. Then she saw . . . a flash of light. A giant ball of fire streaked across the inky sky faster than a wink! Faster than a blink.

Judy jumped up. "Stink? Did you . . . did you see that?"

Stink looked up from his map. "See what?"

"The comet! I think Sherlock-Holmes just flew across the sky!"

"I missed it?" Stink wailed. "Wait. What did it look like?"

"Like a red-hot freaky fireball streaking across the sky. Like Fourth of July fireworks. Like five thousand shooting stars."

"No way did you see a comet," said Stink. "Comets are made of ice, not fire. They don't streak across the sky. And a comet has a tail. Did it have a tail?"

Judy shrugged.

"It was probably just a shooting star or a meteor or a fireball or a supernova."

"Or a UFO!" Judy teased.

"Whatever it was, maybe it'll go by again!" Stink said hopefully.

"It will," said Judy. "In about a hundred years."

"A hundred years! I can't wait till I'm a hundred and seven!"

Judy got an idea. "Stink, I know how you can see a comet." She crawled inside the T. P. Club tent. "Don't come in until I say so."

Stink waited for what felt like a hundred and seven years. "Can I come in yet?"

"Not yet."

Stink itched and scratched and waited. "Now?"

"Not yet."

"How about now?"

"No!"

"Did you know the full moon in March is called a Worm Moon?" Stink asked.

Silence.

"There sure is a lot of peace and quiet out here," said Stink.

"You can come in now," said Judy.

Finally! Stink crawled into the tent.
The inside was covered with stars—
glow-in-the-dark star stickers.

"Wow!" Stink gazed up at his own
small sky. "There's the Big Dipper!
And the Little Dipper. Even the
Medium Dipper!"

Judy pointed to a three-star cluster.

"This is Wynken, Blynken, and Nod.
And that's not all," said Judy. She turned
on not one but two flashlights. One
made a fuzzy ball on the tent sky. She
held the other flashlight at an angle to
make a tail.

"It's a comet!" said Stink. "The
Sherlock-Holmes comet!"

When Judy's arms got tired, she turned off the flashlights and crawled inside her sleeping bag. "Show's over. I'm going to bed."

"I didn't get to see the real comet," said Stink, "but I got the next best thing. My own private galaxy. Thanks, Judy."

"Mm-hmm," said a sleepy Judy.

Stink opened the tent flap to peek at the real sky one last time. The stars twinkled like glitter. All of a sudden, a star streaked across the sky.

"A shooting star!" said Stink. "I saw one! For real!"

"Make a wish," mumbled Judy.

Stink closed his eyes and made a wish.

That night, Stink and Judy went to
the Land of Nod under the winking,
blinking stars. If Stink's wish came
true, they would be doing the exact
same thing in another hundred years.

CHAPTER 2
Master of Disaster

Stink raced home from Saturday Science Club. "The sky is falling! The sky is falling!"

Judy looked up from her ant habitat. "Slow down, Chicken Little," said Judy. "What are you saying?"

"The asteroids are coming! The asteroids are coming! I just found out that a giant meteorite landed in

Russia. No lie. And an even bigger one might be headed for Earth."

"Don't worry, Stink. Dad says tons of space junk hits Earth every day."

"*Don't worry?* Tell that to the dinosaurs. There could be a rock out there with *your* name on it. It could be speeding toward Earth right now, going sixty miles per second. *Disaster*oid!"

Judy watched an ant dig a tunnel.

"How can you think about ants at a time like this?" Stink cried. "Any minute you could be squashed like a pancake. Or squished right down to the size of . . . an ant!"

"Ooh, I could be a yellow crazy ant," said Judy. "And you could be an odorous ant. Odorous ants smell like rotting coconuts when you squish them."

"Get serious," said Stink.

"Stink, if an asteroid hits Earth—"

"You said *if.* But it's not *if,* Judy. It's *when.*"

"What can *I* do about it?" asked Judy.

"You can build a net the size of Virginia to catch the asteroid. You can invent an anti-asteroid Blast-o-Matic machine to destroy it before it reaches us. *Blaster*oid!"

"That sounds too much like homework," said Judy.

"*I'm* going to make an asteroid-proof bunker in the basement."

"You hate the basement," said Judy. "Dark. Scary. Spiders."

"I'd rather be bitten by ten hundred spiders than squished to the size of a coconut ant by a killer asteroid."

Stink put on his bike helmet, water wings, and knee pads. He made himself an aluminum-foil cape. *Asteroid Boy!* Asteroid Boy would protect Earth from killer asteroids!

Stink carried a blanket, a flashlight, and a light saber down to the basement. He carried Toady the toad and Astro the guinea pig to the basement. He carried half his room to the basement. He even took the toaster to the basement.

"Mom! Dad!" called Judy. "Stink just moved into the basement."

"He hates the basement," said Mom.

"That's what I said," said Judy.

"Why the basement?" asked Dad.

"To hide from killer asteroids," said Judy. "They're speeding toward Earth this very second."

"Tons of space junk hits Earth every day," said Dad.

"That's what I said you said," said Judy.

"He'll change his mind at the first sign of a spider," said Mom.

"He'll change his mind as soon as it gets dark," said Dad.

Judy and Mouse the cat tiptoed
down the stairs to the stinky
basement. Stink had built a fort out of
boxes and boards, chairs and crates.

"Like my bunker?" Stink asked.
Before Judy could answer, a loud
roaring sound came from outside.
"Did you hear that? A sonic boom!"

"Lawn mower," said Judy.

Next they heard a whooshing
sound.

ASTEROID-FREE
ZONE

"Did you hear that?" said Stink. "A space storm!"

"Washing machine," said Judy.

Stink heard a crash like breaking glass.

"It's here!" Stink cried. "The asteroid has landed!"

"That was Dad. Doing dishes again," said Judy.

"Do you feel hot?" Stink asked. "I feel hot." He peered out the window. "Did the house just shake? Is that a radioactive glow?"

Just then, the lights went out. The basement went dark. Dark as an eclipse. Dark as a black hole.

"This is it! Killer asteroid hits Earth and takes out power grid!" Stink threw on a pair of goggles, grabbed his light saber, and yelled, "Never fear! Asteroid Boy is here!" He pointed to the toaster, which was covered with magnets. "Judy, activate the Anti-Asteroid Magnetic-Repulsion Device!"

"Stink, I think *you're* the asteroid. You have too much stuff plugged in down here. You blew a fuse. Dad's going to blow a fuse, too."

"But . . . we're alive!" said Stink. He fell to his knees in relief. "We survived a giant ball of rock, metal, and dust crashing into Earth at sixty thousand miles per second."

Judy sniffed the air. "I don't smell rotting coconuts. So I guess we didn't get squashed like ants."

Stink ran outside. Judy ran after him.

Stink peered up at the sky with his asteroid-proof X-ray-vision goggles. Stink peered up into the trees. Stink peered down at the grass.

"I need proof," said Stink. "Proof that I survived an asteroid hitting Earth faster than a speeding bullet."

"You're proof, Stink. I'm proof. See? We're not as flat as pancakes."

"Pancakes! That reminds me. I'm hungry."

"Surviving an asteroid attack will do that," said Judy. "Let's ask Mom if she'll make us silver-dollar pancakes."

"*When*," said Stink.

"Huh?"

"Not *if. When.* Ask Mom *when* she's going to make us pancakes."

"Stink, you are the Master of Disaster!" said Judy. "If an asteroid ever hits Earth, I'm calling Asteroid Boy."

"Not *if*," said Asteroid Boy, grinning ear to ear. "*When*."

CHAPTER 3
Albert Einstink

PLOP! A big fat envelope landed on the Moodys' front step.

"It's for me!" said Stink.

"It's for me!" said Judy.

"But it has *my* name on it," said Stink.

Judy stared at the big fat envelope. It was not her mail-order ants.

Stink grabbed the envelope and

tore it open. "It's from the way-official Name-That-Star Company."

"Name-the-What?"

"Name-That-Star. I'm going to have a star named after me."

"Stink, there are a million, billion stars in the galaxy. I don't think they're going to name one for you."

"Yah-huh." He held up the papers. "It's all right here in my star-naming kit. There's a way-official certificate.

Way-official instructions.

And a real-and-actual
photo of my very own
star."

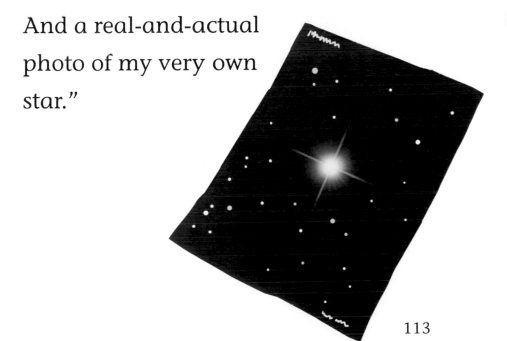

Judy studied the star photo. "Huh. What are you going to name it? *Stink Star?*" She cracked up.

Stink's jaw dropped. "Oh, no," he moaned. "I never thought of that. The Stink Star is not a very good name for a star."

"Use your real name. Call it the James Star."

"*James* is not special enough for a star. There are three Jameses in my second-grade class!"

Judy picked up her Grouchy pencil. "I'll help you. You make a list of names, and I'll make a list of names. Then you'll have tons of names to choose from."

Stink thought and thought. Stink chewed his pencil.

Judy scribbled on her list. "Stella? Stellina? Starla?" she read.

"No girl names," said Stink.

"Orion? Sirius? Hercules?"

"Taken," said Stink.

"Balthazar?"

"Balthazar Moody," said Stink. "Maybe."

Big Head Book of Baby Names

"Let's hear some names on your list," said Judy.

"Batman? Superman? Plutoman?"

"Superman Moody? No way. There's kryptonite in outer space, you know. Your star would get clobbered."

"Spike? Dracula? Godzilla?" Stink asked.

"Dracula Moody. I like it!" said Judy. "But it would starve up there."

Stink got out the *Big Head Book of Baby Names.* "Maybe I'll find a name in here!" He opened to the *A*'s. "Abner, Achilles, Achoo," Stink read.

"Bless you," said Judy.

"No, that's a name: Achoo!"

"No way is somebody named Achoo," said Judy.

Stink frowned. "You're right. My star can't be named for a sneeze."

He flipped some pages. "Sheesh. There are ten hundred names in here. It will take light-years to find the right name."

"Close your eyes, open the book, and point," said Judy.

Stink closed his eyes. Stink opened the book. Stink pointed. "Lollipop,"

he read. "Ten thousand names and I
point to the name of a big slobbery
sucker?"

Stink went to find Mom and Dad. He asked them how to choose a brand-new, not-sneezy, un-slobbery-sucker name to put on a star.

"A name should say something about you," said Mom.

"Like Judy is moody? And Riley Rottenberger is rotten?" asked Stink.

"Sort of," said Dad.

"And like Stink is stinky?" said Judy.

"Try thinking of something that makes you special," said Dad. "Or someone you admire."

Stink's face lit up. "I got it! Albert Einstink!"

"Forget it, Stink Face," said Judy. "Your brain is way too puny."

"How about my initials and my birthday: JEM-229."

"My brother, the robot," said Judy.

"How about a super-cool spy name, like Mosquito? Or Neptune Shadow?"

"That's it!" said Judy.

"Really?"

"N-O!" said Judy. "Let's put all the names in a bowl, Stink. We'll mix them up. Then close your eyes, reach in, and pull one out."

"Hey! You just gave me an idea," said Stink. He scribbled in his notebook. "Ready for this?"

"Ready, Freddy!" said Judy. "Hercules-Balthazar-Superman-Dracula-Achoo-Lollipop-JEM-229-Mosquito-Albert-Einstink."

"You're going to name your star
Hercules-Balthazar-Superman-
Dracula-Achoo-Lollipop-JEM-229-
Mosquito-Albert-Einstink?"
"Right."

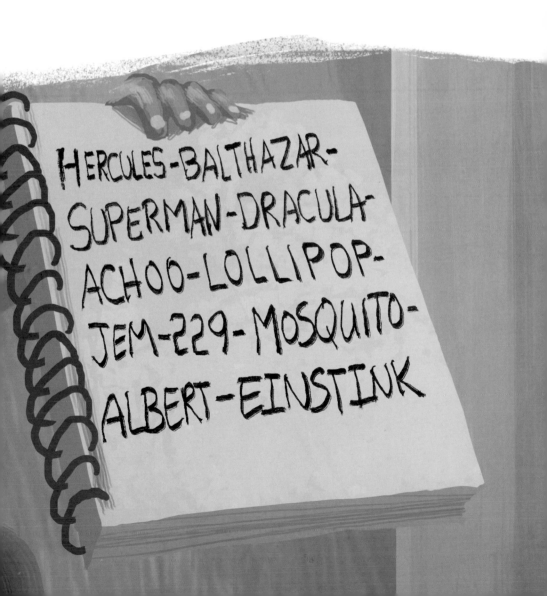

Judy picked up the way-official star packet. She read silently for about a hundred light-years. Then she said, "Stink, there are rules. First of all, a star name can't be more than sixteen letters long. The name you picked is like sixteen million letters long. Plus some numbers!"

"Yikes," said Stink.

"Second of all, a star name can only be one word. Your name is nine million words long."

"Double yikes," said Stink. He scratched his head.

"I know!" he said. "How about if my star's name is Hercules-Balthazar-Superman-Dracula-Achoo-Lollipop-JEM-229-Mosquito-Albert-Einstink, but you call it Stink for short?"

"Perfect," said Mom and Dad.

"You think?" asked Stink.

"If the Stink fits, wear it," said Judy.

Triple Pet Trouble

CONTENTS

CHAPTER 1

Jaws in Love 133

CHAPTER 2

Mystic Mouse 149

CHAPTER 3

Toady and the Vampire 171

CHAPTER 1
Jaws in Love

Jaws looked droopy. Jaws looked mopey. Jaws looked wilty. Jaws was Judy Moody's Venus flytrap. Two of his leaves were turning black. One of his traps was turning dead.

Judy Moody stuck her Grouchy pencil in one of his traps and . . . *snap . . . trap . . . NOT!* Jaws did not snap his trap. Not even when she tried an ant, a tiny cricket, or a roly-poly.

Stink's jaw dropped when he saw Judy's pet. "What's wrong with Jaws? He looks like moldy old bread."

"He's sick," said Judy.

"Ooh. Maybe he has the measles."

"I don't get it," said Judy. "I feed him earwigs from Dad's garden. I take him outside in winter. I snip off his dead leaves when they turn black."

"Maybe he doesn't like his new haircut," said Stink.

"I know," said Judy. "Dr. Judy, Pet Vet, to the rescue!"

Dr. Judy gave Jaws a bath—with rainwater.

She sang him the Baby Bumble Bee song.

She read to him from *Charlotte's Web*.

136

"Don't read him a sad book!" said Stink.

"It's his favorite," said Judy. But Jaws looked as droopy as ever.

Judy looked stuff up in her *Big Head Book of Bug-Eating Plants.* "It says here that there's only one place in the world where Venus flytraps grow in nature."

"Where?"

"A place called Cape Fear," said Judy, "in North Carolina."

Stink shivered. The Moodys' cat, Mouse, pulled her toy mouse in closer. "Maybe Jaws is homesick," said Stink.

"Maybe Jaws is just lonely," Judy said.

"Aha! Jaws needs a friend," said Stink. He ran downstairs and came back carrying a fishbowl. A goldfish was floating on top of the sloshing water.

Stink set the bowl down next to Jaws. "Jaws, meet your new friend, Goldilocks."

Judy peered into the bowl. "Stink. That's no goldfish. That's a cracker. A goldfish-shaped cracker."

"Jaws doesn't know that," whispered Stink.

"He'd probably rather *eat* than *meet* his new friend," Judy whispered back.

Jaws did not perk up one bit.

"It's not working," said Stink.

"Making friends takes time," said Judy.

Judy and Stink gave it time.
One day. Two days. Three days.
Judy peered into the goldfish bowl.
"Goldilocks looks puffy," said Judy,
"and pale."

"Let me see," said Stink, pulling the
fishbowl toward him. The cracker fell
to pieces. "Argh! Jaws's new friend
just became five friends!" cried Stink.

"Jaws looks worse," said Judy.

"You'd look bad, too, if your best friend just turned into Cream of Goldfish," said Stink.

"Let's move Jaws over to the window," said Judy. "I think he needs more light."

They set Jaws down on the window seat next to Mouse and a pile of papers and junk. "Move over, Mouse," said Judy. "Make way for Jaws."

Mouse leaped to the floor, but a piece of paper got stuck to her paw. Junk mail! Mouse shook her paw, trying to get rid of it.

"Mouse is trying to show us something," said Stink.

Judy unstuck the piece of junk mail from Mouse's paw. On the flyer were pictures of a Venus flytrap, a pitcher plant, a sundew, and a cobra lily. *Carnivore city!*

The flyer said GRAND OPENING! The flyer said that a store called Cape Fear Carnivores was opening right there in Frog Neck Lake!

Judy kissed her cat on the nose. She, Dr. Judy Moody, knew just what to do to save Jaws.

Judy and her dad took Jaws to Cape Fear Carnivores. Judy talked to the owner, Peter Tomato. Peter Tomato knew everything in the world about bug-eating plants.

Peter Tomato helped Judy start her very own bog. First she picked out a pot that looked like a mini bathtub. Next she filled it with sand and peat moss. Then she planted Jaws in the bog next to a brand-new, way-tall, red-and-green North American pitcher plant.

"Jaws," said Judy, "meet Petunia, your new bug-eating buddy!"

When Judy and Jaws and Petunia got home, Stink peered into one of the pitcher plant's long tubes.

"There's water in there," said Stink, "and a dead fly."

"That's how a pitcher plant traps its food," said Judy. "An insect smells nectar, lands on the mouth of the plant, and—*zoom*—falls right down into the tube."

"Cool," said Stink.

"Did you know some pitcher plants eat animal poop? They like shrew poo."

"Hardee-har-har," said Stink. "You made that up."

"Did not!" said Judy. "Peter Tomato at Cape Fear Carnivores told me. Peter Tomato would not lie."

Judy sat back to admire her bog. Jaws did not look droopy or mopey or wilty. Jaws looked positively perky.

At last, Jaws had company. He curled a leaf around Petunia, the pitcher plant.

"Look," said Judy. "I think Jaws is in love!"

"Love at first sight," said Stink.

"Love at first bite," said Judy.

CHAPTER 2
Mystic Mouse

Judy was reading to Mouse from her *Big Head Book of Pets.* She was reading all about parrots and potbellied pigs and pocket pets—pets that can fit in a pocket.

Then she looked out the window. "Check it out, Mouse. Stink has a lemonade stand. And his lemonade stand has a big long line."

Jingle-jangle. "I can already hear the jingle of all the quarters in Stink's pockets."

All of a sudden, she, Judy Moody, had an idea. A pockets-full-of-quarters idea.

She set up a table down the sidewalk from Stink. She hung up a sign. She put out an empty jar. She hid her *Big Head Book of Pets* under the table, just in case.

"Hey!" said Stink. "This is my corner."

"It's a free country, Stink."

"Why is Mouse wearing a turban and sitting on your mood pillow like a queen?"

PET PSYCHIC:
Mouse the
Mind Reader

Judy pointed to her sign. PET
PSYCHIC: MOUSE THE MIND READER.
"Mouse knows what other pets are
thinking. She knew Jaws needed a
friend, remember?"

"What's the jar for?"

"The jar is for when all the quarters
start to roll in. Twenty-five cents a
reading."

Stink went back to his table. "Ice-cold lemonade!" cried Stink. "Hand-stirred. Only twenty-five cents!"

"Meet pet psychic Mouse Moody!" called Judy. "Got a pet problem? Mouse can solve it!"

Kids gawked at Mouse on their way to get lemonade but didn't stop. Judy put up more signs. FREE TUMMY RUBS! FREE HEAD SCRATCHES!

FREE TUMMY RUBS!

PET PSYCHIC: Mouse the Mind Reader

Rocky was first in line. "Hi, Rock," said Judy. "What's your pet problem?"

Rocky held out his pet iguana. "It's Houdini. He turned a weird color. And his skin is peeling."

Judy ducked under the table to peek at her Big Head book in secret. She sprang back up and leaned over her cat. "Mouse the Mind Reader

FREE
HEAD
SCRATCHES!

has spoken. She says Houdini is just growing. That's why he's shedding his skin." Judy scratched the back of the iguana's head. "Give him a nice bath, mist him every morning, and he'll feel better."

"Thanks!" said Rocky.

"Twenty-five cents, please," said Judy. *Ka-ching!*

Behind Rocky was Frank Pearl. His parrot, Cookie, sat on his shoulder.

Judy gave Cookie a free tummy rub while Frank told Judy the problem. "My parrot hates my sister," said Frank. "Every time my sister gets too close, Cookie bites her."

"Let me ask Mouse the Mind Reader," said Judy.

"I think your mind reader is sleeping," said Frank.

FREE
TUMMY
RUBS!

PET PSYCHIC:
Mouse the
Mind Reader

"She's not sleeping. She's thinking," said Judy, putting her ear up to Mouse.

"Mouse the Magnificent says it's all about the treats. Do a fun trick with Cookie, but let *your sister* give her a treat."

"Mouse told you all that?" said Frank. "Wow!" He dropped a quarter in the jar.

FREE
HEAD
SCRATCHES!

Next in line were Amy Namey and Jessica Finch. "I don't have a pet," said Amy.

Mouse curled her tail into a question mark. Judy said, "Mouse the Magnificent says, How about a pocket pet? Sugar gliders are cute. They fit in your pocket. Or a goldfish. *Not* the cracker kind. Twenty-five cents, please."

"But I'm not here about a pet for me," said Amy. "I'm here about PeeGee." She pointed to Jessica Finch's potbellied pig on a leash.

"PeeGee is freaking out," Jessica told Judy. "Every time he comes into my room, he knocks over my chair and chews my shoes and squeals like a—"

"Pig?" asked Judy.

Jessica nodded.

"Got that, Mouse?" Judy said. Mouse purred. Mouse purred some more.

"Mouse is thinking," said Judy.

"How do you know what she's thinking?" asked Jessica.

"Mouse and I are of one mind. It sounds to me—I mean to Mouse—like *somebody* needs to learn a few rules at obedience school."

"I love rules!" said Jessica. "And obedience. Maybe I can teach PeeGee myself."

Clink. Clink. Clink-clink-clink. The quarters kept on coming.

Mouse helped a parakeet with no tweet (Hello! Turn on the light),

a fish with ick, a.k.a. measles (Hello! Get fish medicine from the pet store),

and a pet rock that lost one googly
eye (Hello, glue!).

Mouse was a regular Dr. Dolittle,
an animal whisperer of the third
kind, a pet psychic with a sixth sense.

Judy jingled and jangled the
quarters in her jar for Stink to hear.

"Hey!" said Stink. "You're stealing
all my customers. Everybody wants
to see Mouse the Mystic. Nobody's
thirsty anymore."

Judy held up Mouse's water bowl for everyone to see. "Mouse the Mystic will now gaze into the Eternal Water Bowl of Serenity."

FREE TUMMY RUBS!

PET PSYCHIC: Mouse the ___ Reader

FREE HEAD SCRATCHES!

Mouse twitched her whiskers. Mouse licked her lips. "Mouse feels a great thirst coming on," said Judy.

Mouse stuck out her tongue and lapped up water like crazy.

A hush fell over the crowd. Everyone gazed at Mouse the Mind Reader.

"Come to think of it," said Frank, "I feel thirsty, too."

"Me, too," said Rocky and Amy at the same time.

"Me, three," said Jessica Finch. "PeeGee's thirsty, too."

Now everybody rushed to get in line at Stink's table. In two minutes flat, Stink ran out of lemonade. He ran into the house and came back carrying a pitcher of water.

LEMONADE

"Ice-cold water!" Stink yelled. "From the Eternal Fountain of Thirst Quenching. Hand-stirred! Only twenty-five cents a cup!"

CHAPTER 3
Toady and the Vampire

Zing! Toady zinged off Judy's bottom bunk bed. *Boing!* He boinged off her finger-knitting yarn. Stink's pet toad, Toady, was going nutso, zinging and boinging all over the place.

Judy scooped him up, then squished into her window seat between Mouse and the bog buddies, Jaws and Petunia.

EEW! All of a sudden, Judy felt something warm and wet in her hand. *Gross-o-rama!* She set the toad down.

Toady made a puddle on her mood pillow. "Bad Toady!" Judy said.

Then he made a puddle on top of her gumball machine. "Bad, bad Toady!" Judy said.

He made a puddle in the middle of
her squiggle rug.

"That does it!" said Judy. "You and I
are going on a field trip."

Judy rode Toady to Jessica Finch's
house on her bike. A sign in the yard
said JESSICA FINCH'S DOGGY DAY CARE
AND OBEDIENCE SCHOOL.

JESSICA FINCH'S
DOGGY
DAY CARE
AND
OBEDIENCE
SCHOOL

Judy did not see a single dog. She did see Houdini, Rocky's iguana; Cookie, Frank's parrot; and PeeGee WeeGee, Jessica's pig, running around like crazy. Jessica was shouting, "Sit," "Stay," and "Heel," but none of them listened. None of them behaved.

This looked more like DIS-obedience school!

Jessica Finch and Amy Namey ran over to Judy. A stripe-faced fur ball with dark eyes and a pink nose stuck its head out of Amy's pocket. "Meet Boo," said Amy. "It's short for Peek-a-Boo."

"You got a sugar glider?" asked Judy. "You lucky dog!"

"How come *you're* here?" Jessica asked Judy.

"Toady's being a bad toad today." Judy told them about the toad pee on everything. "Will you take one more student?"

Jessica frowned. Jessica hemmed and hawed.

"Don't be a toadstool," said Judy.

"Okay. He can stay."

"Sit!" Jessica said to the animals. Houdini crawled away.

"Sit!" Jessica said again. Cookie hopped up and down and clacked her beak.

"Sit!" PeeGee just chased his tail.

"Sit!" Boo jumped out of Amy's pocket and knocked over his barrel of toy monkeys.

"Sit!" said Jessica. Toady sat.

Judy clapped her hands. "Toady!
You did it!"

"Stay!" said Jessica. Houdini crawled under a pile of leaves.

"Stay!" Jessica called again. Cookie flapped her wings and flew onto Judy's head.

"Stay!" PeeGee chased his tail some more.

"Stay!" Boo glided through the air and landed on PeeGee.

"Stay!" Jessica told Toady. Toady stayed.

"Good Toady!" Judy yelled.

Jessica held up a Hula-Hoop.
"Jump!" she said. PeeGee
chased after a ball. "Bad pig!"
yelled Jessica. Boo chased
after PeeGee. Cookie chased
after Boo.

Jessica tried again. "Jump!"
Toady jumped . . . right
through the Hula-Hoop!

"You're good at getting Toady to obey," said Judy.

"Gold star for you, Toady." Jessica held him in her hand. "I still want to be in your Toad Pee Club," she said to the toad, "but you won't even pee on me."

"Toady gets an A-plus for Toad School," said Judy.

"That'll be one dollar," said Jessica Finch.

"Will you take four quarters?" Judy asked.

The next day, Judy teased Toady about obedience school. "You are *toadally* teacher's pet!" she said. All of a sudden, she felt something warm and wet on her hand. *Eew!* That naughty toad sprang out of her hand and hopped under the bed.

Judy heard a voice. "Hey, Judy! Want to go monster hunting?" It was Amy Namey.

"I *am* monster hunting," said Judy. She rescued Toady and dusted him off. "*This* monster. Toady acted perfect at obedience school. But the second I got him home, he turned into a little monster again. I don't get it."

Amy wasn't listening. Amy was staring. Amy was pointing at Judy's

new plant on the window seat. "You have a pitcher plant? I saw one in Borneo. It had one of those long scary names like *Carnivoria vampira* or something."

"This isn't a vampire," said Judy. "This is a new friend for Jaws. Her name is Petunia."

"Uh-oh," said Amy.

"What-oh?" asked Judy. She set Toady down on her top bunk.

"Um, I hate to tell you this, but . . . some giant pitcher plants can eat a frog."

Judy sprang up. *A frog-eating pitcher plant? Gulp!*

"Or a mouse or a rat," said Amy, "or a . . . *toad!*"

"No wonder Toady's been acting psycho," said Judy. "He's scared of Petunia, the vampire pitcher plant!"

Judy turned to look at Toady—
Wait! Toady? Where was that toad now?

Judy rushed over to Petunia. "Open wide and say 'Ahh'!" Judy said in her best doctor voice. She looked down Petunia's throat.

Judy did not see a bug. She did not see a spider, ant, or earwig. She saw a puddle. A small puddle of liquid. Amy saw it, too.

Was it . . . could it be . . . toad pee?

"ROAR!" said Judy. "The vampire plant ate Toady!"

Just then, Stink came running into Judy's room. "*Who* ate Toady?" he asked.

"Nobody."

"Where is he, then?"

"Um . . ." said Judy.

Just then, Toady hopped from the bedpost to the desk to the doorknob.

"Right there," said Amy, pointing.

Stink scooped him up. "Phew. Don't scare me like that."

Judy pushed Stink and Toady toward the door. "Stink! Get him out of here! My room is now officially a FROG-FREE zone."

"A toad is not a frog," said Stink.

"Tell that to the *Toadivoria vampira!*" said Judy.

"The *toadi*-huh?"

Judy pointed to the pitcher plant. "Stink, I hate to tell you this. But Jaws's new BFF is a freaky, frog-eating vampire. No lie. Say hello to Count Petunia."

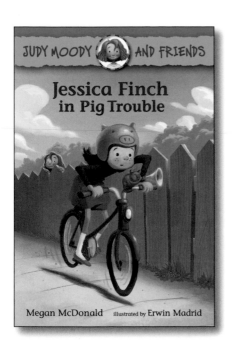

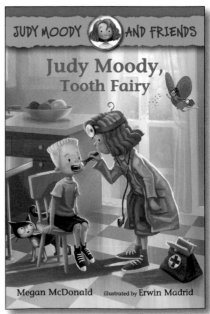

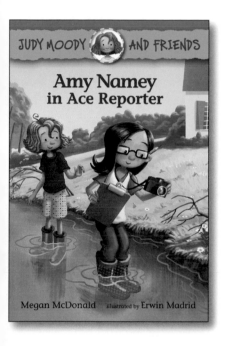

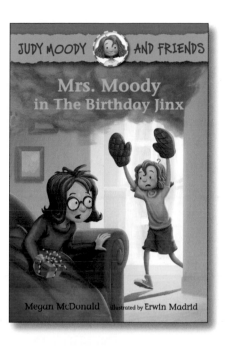

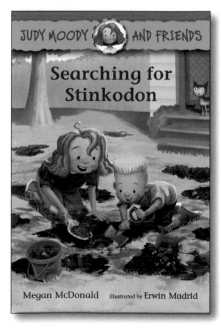

Megan McDonald is the author of the popular Judy Moody and Stink series for older readers. She has also written many other books for children, including two books for beginning readers: *Ant and Honey Bee: A Pair of Friends at Halloween* and *Ant and Honey Bee: A Pair of Friends in Winter.* Megan McDonald lives in California.

Erwin Madrid has worked as a visual development artist for the Shrek franchise and *Madagascar: Escape 2 Africa* and has created conceptual art for video games. He is also the illustrator of *The Scary Places Map Book* by B. G. Hennessy. Erwin Madrid lives in California.